Dear Parents and Educators,

Welcome to Penguin Young Readers! As parents and educators, you know that each child develops at his or her own pace—in terms of speech, critical thinking, and, of course, reading. Penguin Young Readers recognizes this fact. As a result, each Penguin Young Readers book is assigned a traditional easy-to-read level (1–4) as well as a Guided Reading Level (A–P). Both of these systems will help you choose the right book for your child. Please refer to the back of each book for specific leveling information. Penguin Young Readers features esteemed authors and illustrators, stories about favorite characters, fascinating nonfiction, and more!

Miss Bindergarten and the Very Wet Day

LEVEL 2

GUIDED READING LEVEL **E**

This book is perfect for a **Progressing Reader** who:
- can figure out unknown words by using picture and context clues;
- can recognize beginning, middle, and ending sounds;
- can make and confirm predictions about what will happen in the text; and
- can distinguish between fiction and nonfiction.

Here are some **activities** you can do during and after reading this book:
- Make Connections: Miss B likes both the sun and rain because together they can make a rainbow. Discuss different kinds of weather. Which type is your favorite? Why?
- Sight Words: Sight words are frequently used words that readers must know just by looking at them. These words are not "sounded out" or "decoded"; rather they are known instantly, on sight. Knowing these words helps children develop into efficient readers. As you read the story, have the child point out the sight words listed below.

all	has	look	they
and	her	now	will
are	here	put	you

Remember, sharing the love of reading with a child is the best gift you can give!

—Bonnie Bader, EdM
  Penguin Young Readers program

*Penguin Young Readers are leveled by independent reviewers applying the standards developed by Irene Fountas and Gay Su Pinnell in *Matching Books to Readers: Using Leveled Books in Guided Reading*, Heinemann, 1999.

For Elaeth Ki Duk Kirk, going on two—JS

For Maria Thayer, may your
rain barrels always be full—AW

PENGUIN YOUNG READERS
An Imprint of Penguin Random House LLC

Text copyright © 2015 by Joseph Slate. Illustrations copyright © 2015 by Ashley Wolff. All rights reserved.
Published by Penguin Young Readers, an imprint of Penguin Random House LLC, 345 Hudson Street,
New York, New York 10014. Manufactured in China.

Library of Congress Cataloging-in-Publication Data is available.

ISBN 978-0-448-48700-7 (pbk)   10 9 8 7 6 5 4 3 2
ISBN 978-0-448-48701-4 (hc)   10 9 8 7 6 5 4 3 2 1

PENGUIN YOUNG READERS

LEVEL
2
PROGRESSING
READER

Miss Bindergarten
and the Very Wet Day

WITHDRAWN

by Joseph Slate
illustrated by Ashley Wolff

Penguin Young Readers
An Imprint of Penguin Random House

Meet Miss Bindergarten.

Here is her class.

They call her Miss B.

One day at school,

the rain is falling.

It is a very wet day.

Coco is wet.

Coco is cold.

"Poor Coco," says Patty.

"We will dry you," says Matty.

Now Coco is warm.

The rain falls all day.

The day is dark.

The day is cold.

But later, Matty looks out.

"Look, Miss B," says Matty.

"The rain has stopped."

"Now we can go out to play,"

says Miss B.

"Put on your coats.

Put on your boots."

"Look," says Patty.

"There is a big puddle!"

"I will jump over it," says Matty.

Oh no!

Matty falls down.

Matty is all wet.

"I will help you," says Patty.

Oh no!

Patty falls down, too.

Patty is all wet!

Coco and Miss B help Patty

and Matty.

"Oh no," says Matty.

"It has started to rain."

"But look," says Patty.

"The sun is out, too."

"I like the sun," says Matty.

"It is warm."

"I like the sun, too," says Patty.

"It is yellow."

"I like the sun AND the rain,"

says Miss B.

"The sun and the rain can make

a rainbow!"